Pie in the Sky

Lois Ehlert

Harcourt, Inc.

Orlando   Austin   New York   San Diego   Toronto   London

Manufactured in China

W9-APC-451

DATE DUE		
JUN 1 4 2004	SEP 0 1 2015	
AUG 1 0 200?		
SEP 0 2 200? JAN 1-9 2016		
AUG 0 4 200? DEC 0 7 2016		
APR 1 0 2010		
...? 1 ? 2010 NOV 0 1 2017		
NOV 0 ?? 2010 OCT 0 6 2018		
SEP 1 9 2011		
DEC 2 0 2012		
OCT 0 8 2013		
DEC 1 7 2014		
APR 1 1 2015		

This tree
was here when
we moved in.

Dad says it's
a pie tree.

I see
a blue jay feather
with black stripes
and a white tip,
and a green caterpillar
with a yellow band
and an orange false eye.
But no pie.

I've never seen pies growing on trees. Wouldn't that be something?

I see
green grass,
red ladybugs,
red brown bark,
and a blue green
dragonfly.
But no pie.

Dad showed me buds on our tree today. He says that's a good sign, but we won't know till summer if we'll get pie.

I see yellow leaves
with green spots,
brown buds,
a brown chrysalis,
and a gray snow sky.
But no pie.

Winter's finally over. Sweet spring is here at last. Buds we saw last fall are bursting into bloom.

I see
green leaves,
white blossoms,
yellow pollen dust,
blue eggs
in a brown nest,
yellow honeybees,
and black stripes
on a yellow
butterfly.
But no pie.

But now a damp wind
is blowing, and all
the flower petals
are falling down
like rain.

I see
white petals,
dark gray tails,
brown branches,
and a gray rain sky.
But no pie.

You know what? I think something's finally growing on that tree of ours.

I see orange and lime green balls, yellow moon and stars, a pàle green moth, and a dark blue sky. But no pie.

The birds sure
sound excited.
I wonder what's
going on.

I see
a robin's rusty red breast
and white-speckled throat,
a gray catbird with a
black crown and tail,
and purple-violet clouds
in a pink-and-orange sky.
But no pie.

Uh-oh.

Now
I see.

I see
brown cherry pits,
red wing tips
on cedar waxwings,
and white rings
around robins'
black eyes.
But no pies.

It's a
cherry
feast!

I see
orange-breasted
orioles,
black spots and tips
on butterfly wings,
red ripe cherries,
and a bright blue sky.
But no pie.

But, hey, raccoon,
save some
for us!

I see
a raccoon's black mask,
black toes,
black nose and eye,
and the
lime green glow
of fireflies.
But no pies.

At last
Dad says it's
time for *us*
to pick
cherries.

I see
gray wings,
a black-and-orange tail,
a yellow beak,
a silver gray pail,
and a blue fly.
Still no pie.

We're
going
to make
a pie!

First we wash
the cherries.

4 cups
sour
red
cherries

We squeeze out all the pits

and save the juice.

Then we put the
cherries in a bowl.

½ cup juice

We add the juice,
flour, sugar, and
cinnamon,
and stir it with
a spoon.

5 tbsp. flour

1/3 cups sugar

1/2 tsp. cinnamon

Next we mix
the piecrust
dough.

We roll out two crusts
and press one
in the pan.

Then we pour the filling in.

9-inch pan

We add
the top crust,
put the pie
in the oven,

and
wait
for it
to bake.

Press around crust edge with a fork to seal.

Cut design into crust so steam can escape while baking.

Preheat oven to 450°. Bake 10 minutes.

Reduce heat to 350°. Bake 35 to 45 minutes, until brown.

Now
Dad
cuts the pie.

He
puts
a piece
on each plate.

Wow!
That was
the best pie
I've ever
eaten.

I wonder if the birds would like it?